Bret Harte

East and West Poems

Bret Harte

East and West Poems

ISBN/EAN: 9783744773157

Printed in Europe, USA, Canada, Australia, Japan

Cover: Foto ©Andreas Hilbeck / pixelio.de

More available books at **www.hansebooks.com**

EAST AND WEST

POEMS.

BY

BRET HARTE.

BOSTON:
JAMES R. OSGOOD AND COMPANY,
(LATE TICKNOR & FIELDS, AND FIELDS, OSGOOD, & CO.)
1871.

CONTENTS.

I.

II.

PART I.

EAST AND WEST POEMS.

A GREYPORT LEGEND.

(1797.)

THEY ran through the streets of the seaport town ;

They peered from the decks of the ships that lay:

The cold sea-fog that came whitening down

Was never as cold or white as they.

"Ho, Starbuck and Pinckney and Tenterden !

Run for your shallops, gather your men,

Scatter your boats on the lower bay."

7

Good cause for fear! In the thick midday

The hulk that lay by the rotting pier,

Filled with the children in happy play,

Parted its moorings, and drifted clear, —

    Drifted clear beyond the reach or call, —

    Thirteen children they were in all, —

      All adrift in the lower bay!

Said a hard-faced skipper, "God help us all!

She will not· float till the turning tide!"

Said his wife, "My darling will hear *my* call,

Whether in sea or heaven she bide:"

    And she lifted a quavering voice and high,

    Wild and strange as a sea-bird's cry,

      Till they shuddered and wondered at her side.

The fog drove down on each laboring crew,

Veiled each from each and the sky and shore:

There was not a sound but the breath they drew,

And the lap of water and creak of oar;

    And they felt the breath of the downs, fresh blown

    O'er leagues of clover and cold gray stone,

      But not from the lips that had gone before.

They come no more. But they tell the tale,

That, when fogs are thick on the harbor reef,

The mackerel fishers shorten sail;

For the signal they know will bring relief:

    For the voices of children, still at play

    In a phantom hulk that drifts alway

      Through channels whose waters never fail.

It is but a foolish shipman's tale,

A theme for a poet's idle page ;

But still, when the mists of doubt prevail,

And we lie becalmed by the shores of Age,

We hear from the misty troubled shore

The voice of the children gone before,

Drawing the soul to its anchorage.

A NEWPORT ROMANCE.

THEY say that she died of a broken heart
    (I tell the tale as 'twas told to me) ;
But her spirit lives, and her soul is part
    Of this sad old house by the sea.

                .

Her lover was fickle and fine and French :
    It was nearly a hundred years ago
When he sailed away from her arms — poor wench —
    With the Admiral Rochambeau.

I marvel much what periwigged phrase
    Won the heart of this sentimental Quaker,

At what golden-laced speech of those modish days
　　She listened — the mischief take her !

But she kept the posies of mignonette
　　That he gave ; and ever as their bloom failed
And faded (though with her tears still wet)
　　Her youth with their own exhaled.

Till one night, when the sea-fog wrapped a shroud
　　Round spar and spire and tarn and tree,
Her soul went up on that lifted cloud
　　From this sad old house by the sea.

And ever since then, when the clock strikes two,
　　She walks unbidden from room to room,
And the air is filled that she passes through
　　With a subtle, sad perfume.

The delicate odor of mignonette,

   The ghost of a dead and gone bouquet,

Is all that tells of her story; yet

   Could she think of a sweeter way?

    .   .   .   .   .   .

I sit in the sad old house to-night, —

   Myself a ghost from a farther sea;

And I trust that this Quaker woman might,

   In courtesy, visit me.

For the laugh is fled from porch and lawn,

   And the bugle died from the fort on the hill,

And the twitter of girls on the stairs is gone,

   And the grand piano is still.

Somewhere in the darkness a clock strikes two;

   And there is no sound in the sad old house,

But the long veranda dripping with dew,

    And in the wainscot a mouse.

The light of my study-lamp streams out

    From the library door, but has gone astray

In the depths of the darkened hall. Small doubt

    But the Quakeress knows the way.

Was it the trick of a sense o'erwrought

    With outward watching and inward fret?

But I swear that the air just now was fraught

    With the odor of mignonette!

I open the window, and seem almost —

    So still lies the ocean — to hear the beat

Of its Great Gulf artery off the coast,

    And to bask in its tropic heat.

In my neighbor's windows the gas-lights flare,

  As the dancers swing in a waltz of Strauss ;

And I wonder now could I fit that air

  To the song of this sad old house.

And no odor of mignonette there is

  But the breath of morn on the dewy lawn ;

And mayhap from causes as slight as this

  The quaint old legend is born.

But the soul of that subtle, sad perfume,

  As the spiced embalmings, they say, outlast

The mummy laid in his rocky tomb,

  Awakens my buried past.

And I think of the passion that shook my youth,

  Of its aimless loves and its idle pains,

And am thankful now for the certain truth

    That only the sweet remains.

And I hear no rustle of stiff brocade,

    And I see no face at my library door ;

For now that the ghosts of my heart are laid,

    She is viewless forevermore.

But whether she came as a faint perfume,

    Or whether a spirit in stole of white,

I feel, as I pass from the darkened room,

    She has been with my soul to-night !

THE HAWK'S NEST.

(SIERRAS.)

WE checked our pace, — the red road sharply round-

  ing ;

  We heard the troubled flow

Of the dark olive depths of pines, resounding

  A thousand feet below.

Above the tumult of the cañon lifted,

  The gray hawk breathless hung ;

Or on the hill a wingèd shadow drifted

  Where furze and thorn-bush clung ;

2*

Or where half-way the mountain side was furrowed
  With many a seam and scar ;
Or some abandoned tunnel dimly burrowed, —
  A mole-hill seen so far.

We looked in silence down across the distant
  Unfathomable reach :
A silence broken by the guide's consistent
  And realistic speech.

"Walker of Murphy's blew a hole through Peters
  For telling him he lied ;
Then up and dusted out of South Hornitos
  Across the long Divide.

" We ran him out of Strong's, and up through Eden,
  And 'cross the ford below ;

And up this cañon (Peters' brother leadin'),
    And me and Clark and Joe.

" He fou't us game : somehow, I disremember
    Jest how the-thing kem round ;
Some say 'twas wadding, some a scattered ember
    From fires on the ground.

" But in one minute all the hill below him
    Was just one sheet of flame ;
Guardin' the crest, Sam Clark and I called to him.
    And, — well, the dog was game !

" He made no sign : the fires of hell were round him,
    The pit of hell below.
We sat and waited, but never found him ;
    And then we turned to go.

"And then — you see that rock that's grown so
        bristly
    With chaparral and tan —
Suthin' crep' out: it might hev been a grizzly,
    It might hev been a man ;

"Suthin' that howled, and gnashed its teeth, and
        shouted
    In smoke and dust and flame ;
Suthin' that sprang into the depths about it,
    Grizzly or man, — but game !

"That's all. Well, yes, it does look rather risky,
    And kinder makes one queer
And dizzy looking down. A drop of whiskey
    Ain't a bad thing right here ! "

IN THE MISSION GARDEN.

(1865.)

FATHER FELIPE.

I SPEAK not the English well, but Pachita

She speak for me ; is it not so, my Pancha ?

Eh, little rogue ? Come, salute me the stranger

Americano.

Sir, in my country we say, "Where the heart is,

There live the speech." Ah ! you not understand ? So !

Pardon an old man, — what you call "ol fogy," —

Padre Felipe !

21

Old, Señor, old! just so old as the Mission.

You see that pear-tree? How old you think, Señor?

Fifteen year? Twenty? Ah, Señor, just *Fifty*

     Gone since I plant him!

You like the wine? It is some at the Mission,

Made from the grape of the year Eighteen Hundred;

All the same time when the earthquake he come to

     San Juan Bautista.

But Pancha is twelve, and she is the rose-tree;

And I am the olive, and this is the garden:

And Pancha we say; but her name is Francisca,

     Same like her mother.

Eh, you knew *her?* No? Ah! it is a story;

But I speak not, like Pachita, the English:

So? If I try, you will sit here beside me,

>   And shall not laugh, eh?

When the American come to the Mission,

Many arrive at the house of Francisca :

One, — he was fine man, — he buy the cattle

>   Of José Castro.

So! he came much, and Francisca she saw him :

And it was Love, — and a very dry season ;

And the pears bake on the tree, — and the rain come,

>   But not Francisca ;

Not for one year; and one night I have walk much

Under the olive-tree, when comes Francisca:

Comes to me here, with her child, this Francisca, —

Under the olive-tree.

Sir, it was sad; ... but I speak not the English;

So! ... she stay here, and she wait for her husband:

He come no more, and she sleep on the hillside;

There stands Pachita.

Ah! there's the Angelus.   Will you not enter?

Or shall you walk in the garden with Pancha?

Go, little rogue — stt — attend to the stranger.

Adios, Señor.

PACHITA (*briskly*).

So, he's been telling that yarn about mother!

Bless you, he tells it to every stranger:

Folks about yer say the old 'man's my father;

What's your opinion?

2

THE OLD MAJOR EXPLAINS.

(RE-UNION ARMY OF THE POTOMAC, 12TH MAY, 1871.)

"WELL, you see, the fact is, Colonel, I don't know as

    I can come:

For the farm is not half planted, and there's work to

    do at home;

And my leg is getting troublesome,—it laid me up

    last fall,

And the doctors, they have cut and hacked, and never

    found the ball.

26

"And then, for an old man like me, it's not exactly

right,

This kind o' playing soldier with no enemy in sight.

'The Union,'—that was well enough way up to '66 ;

But this 'Re-Union,'—maybe now it's mixed with

politics ?

"No ? Well, you understand it best ; but then, you

see, my lad,

I'm deacon now, and some might think that the exam-

ple's bad.

And week from next is Conference. . . . You said the

12th of May ?

Why, that's the day we broke their line at Spottsyl-

van-i-a !

"Hot work; eh, Colonel, wasn't it? Ye mind that
    narrow front:
They called it the 'Death-Angle!' Well, well, my
    lad, we won't
Fight that old battle over now: I only meant to say
I really can't engage to come upon the 12th of May.

"How's Thompson? What! will he be there? Well,
    now, I want to know!
The first man in the rebel works! they called him
    'Swearing Joe:'
A wild young fellow, sir, I fear the rascal was; but
    then —
Well, short of heaven, there wa'n't a place he dursn't
    lead his men.

"And Dick, you say, is coming too.   And Billy?
    ah! it's true

We buried him at Gettysburg: I mind the spot; do
    you?

A little field below the hill, — it must be green this
    May;

Perhaps that's why the fields about bring him to me
    to-day.

" Well, well, excuse me, Colonel! but there are some
    things that drop

The tail-board out one's feelings; and the only way's
    to stop.

So they want to see the old man; ah, the rascals! do
    they, eh?

Well, I've business down in Boston about the 12th of
    May."

"SEVENTY-NINE."

MR. INTERVIEWER INTERVIEWED.

Know me next time when you see me, won't you, old

smarty ?

Oh, I mean you, old figger-head, — just the same

party !

Take out your pensivil, d—n you ; sharpen it, do !

Any complaints to make ?   Lots of 'em — one of

'em's *you.*

You! who are you, anyhow, goin' round in that
  sneakin' way?

Never in jail before, was you, old blatherskite, say?

Look at it; don't it look pooty? Oh, grin, and be
  d—d to you, do!

But, if I had you this side o' that gratin', I'd just make
  it lively for you.

How did I get in here? Well, what 'ud you give to
  know?

'Twasn't by sneakin' round where I hadn't no call
  to go:

'Twasn't by hangin' round a spyin' unfortnet men.

Grin! but I'll stop your jaw if ever you do that
  . agen.

Why don't you say suthin', blast you ?   Speak your
 mind if you dare.

Ain't I a bad lot, sonny ?   Say it, and call it square.

Hain't got no tongue, hey, hev ye.   O guard ! here's
 a little swell,

A cussin' and swearin' and yellin', and bribin' me not
 to tell.

There, I thought that 'ud fetch ye.   And you want to
 know my name ?

" Seventy-Nine " they call me ; but that is their little
 game.

For I'm werry highly connected, as a gent, sir, can
 understand ;

And my family hold their heads up with the very furst
 in the land.

For 'twas all, sir, a put-up job on a pore young man
like me ;

And the jury was bribed a puppos, and aftdrst they
couldn't agree.

And I sed to the judge, sez I, — Oh, grin ! it's all
right my son !

But you're a werry lively young pup, and you ain't to
be played upon !

Wot's that you got — tobacco ? I'm cussed but I
thought 'twas a tract.

Thank ye. A chap t'other day — now, look'ee, this
is a fact,

Slings me a tract on the evils o' keepin' bad company,

As if all the saints was howlin' to stay here
along 's we.

No : I hain't no complaints. Stop, yes ; do you see
  that chap, —

Him standin' over there, — a hidin' his eyes in his
  cap ?

Well, that man's stumick is weak, and he can't stand
  the pris'n fare ;

For the coffee is just half beans, and the sugar ain't
  no where.

Perhaps it's his bringin' up ; but he sickens day
  by day,

And he doesn't take no food, and I'm seein' him waste
  away.

And it isn't the thing to see ; for, whatever he's been
  and done,

Starvation isn't the plan as he's to be saved upon.

For he cannot rough it like me; and he hasn't the
stamps, I guess,

To buy him his extry grub outside o' the pris'n mess.

And perhaps if a gent like you, with whom I've been
sorter free,

Would — thank you! But, say, look here! Oh, blast
it, don't give it to ME!

Don't you give it to me; now, don't ye, don't ye,
don't!

You think it's a put-up job; so I'll thank ye, sir, if
you won't.

But hand him the stamps yourself: why, he isn't even
my pal;

And if it's a comfort to you, why, I don't intend that
he shall.

HIS ANSWER TO " HER LETTER."

REPORTED BY TRUTHFUL JAMES.

BEING asked by an intimate party, —
    Which the same I would term as a friend, —
Which his health it were vain to call hearty,
    Since the mind to deceit it might lend ;
For his arm it was broken quite recent,
    And has something gone wrong with his lung, —
Which is why it is proper and decent
    I should write what he runs off his tongue :

36

First, he says, Miss, he's read through your letter

    To the end,—and the end came too soon ;

That a slight illness kept him your debtor

    (Which for weeks he was wild as a loon) ;

That his spirits are buoyant as yours is ;

    That with you, Miss, he challenges Fate

(Which the language that invalid uses

    At times it were vain to relate).

And he says that the mountains are fairer

    For once being held in your thought ;

That each rock holds a wealth that is rarer

    Than ever by gold-seeker sought

(Which are words he would put in these pages,

    By a party not given to guile ;

Which the same not, at date, paying wages,

    Might produce in the sinful a smile).

4

He remembers the ball at the Ferry,

 And the ride, and the gate, and the vow,

And the rose that you gave him, — that very

 Same rose he is treasuring now

(Which his blanket he's kicked on his trunk, Miss,

 And insists on his legs being free ;

And his language to me from his bunk, Miss,

 Is frequent and painful and free) ;

He hopes you are wearing no willows,

 But are happy and gay all the while ;

That he knows (which this dodging of pillows

 Imparts but small ease to the style,

And the same you will pardon), — he knows, Miss,

 That, though parted by many a mile,

Yet were he lying under the snows, Miss,

 They'd melt into tears at your smile.

And you'll still think of him in your pleasures,

　In your brief twilight dreams of the past;

In this green laurel-spray that he treasures,

　It was plucked where your parting was last;

In this specimen, — but a small trifle, —

　It will do for a pin for your shawl

(Which the truth not to wickedly stifle

　Was his last week's "clean up," — and *his all*).

He's asleep, which the same might seem strange, Miss,

　Were it not that I scorn to deny

That I raised his last dose, for a change, Miss,

　In view that his fever was high;

But he lies there quite peaceful and pensive.

　And now, my respects, Miss, to you;

Which my language, although comprehensive,

　Might seem to be freedom, — it's true.

Which I have a small favor to ask you,

   As concerns a bull-pup, which the same, —

If the duty would not overtask you, —

   You would please to procure for me, *game;*

And send per express to the Flat, Miss,

   Which they say York is famed for the breed,

Which though words of deceit may be that, Miss,

   I'll trust to your taste, Miss, indeed.

P.S. — Which this same interfering

   Into other folks' way I despise ;

Yet if it so be I was hearing

   That it's just empty pockets as lies

Betwixt you and Joseph, it follers,

   That, having no family claims,

Here's my pile ; which it's six hundred dollars,

   As is yours, with respects,

                TRUTHFUL JAMES.

FURTHER LANGUAGE FROM TRUTHFUL JAMES.

(NYE'S FORD, STANISLAUS.)

(1870.)

Do I sleep? do I dream?

Do I wonder and doubt?

Are things what they seem?

Or is visions about?

Is our civilization a failure?

Or is the Caucasian played out?

Which expressions are strong;

Yet would feebly imply

Some account of a wrong —

Not to call it a lie —

As was worked off on William, my pardner,

And the same being W. Nye.

He came down to the Ford

On the very same day

Of that lottery drawed

By those sharps at the Bay;

And he says to me, "Truthful, how goes it?"

I replied, "It is far, far from gay;

"For the camp has gone wild

On this lottery game,

And has even beguiled

'Injin Dick' by the same."

Which said Nye to me, "Injins is pizen:

Do you know what his number is, James?"

I replied " 7,2,

9,8,4, is his hand;"

When he started, and drew

Out a list, which he scanned;

Then he softly went for his revolver

With language I cannot command.

Then I said, "William Nye!"

But he turned upon me,

And the look in his eye

Was quite painful to see;   ˋ

And he says, "You mistake: this poor Injin

I protects from such sharps as you be!"

I was shocked and withdrew;

But I grieve to relate,

When he next met my view

Injin Dick was his mate,

And the two around town was a-lying

In a frightfully dissolute state.

Which the war-dance they had

Round a tree at the Bend

Was a sight that was sad;

And it seemed that the end

Would not justify the proceedings,

As I quiet remarked to a friend.

For that Injin he fled

The next day to his band;

And we found William spread

Very loose on the strand,

With a peaceful-like smile on his features,

And a dollar greenback in his hand ;

Which, the same when rolled out,

We observed with surprise,

That that Injin, no doubt,

Had believed was the prize, —

Them figures in red in the corner,

Which the number of notes specifies.

Was it guile, or a dream?

Is it Nye that I doubt?

Are things what they seem?

Or is visions about?

Is our civilization a failure?

Or is the Caucasian played out?

THE WONDERFUL SPRING OF SAN JOAQUIN.

Of all the fountains that poets sing, —

Crystal, thermal, or mineral spring;

Ponce de Leon's Fount of Youth;

Wells with bottoms of doubtful truth;

In short, of all the springs of Time

That ever were flowing in fact or rhyme,

That ever were tasted, felt, or seen, —

There were none like the Spring of San Joaquin.

Anno Domini Eighteen-Seven,

Father Dominguez (now in heaven, —

Obiit, Eighteen twenty-seven)

Found the spring, and found it, too,

By his mule's miraculous cast of a shoe ;

For his beast — a descendant of Balaam's ass —

Stopped on the instant, and would not pass.

The Padre thought the omen good,

And bent his lips to the trickling flood ;

Then — as the chronicles declare,

On the honest faith of a true believer —

His cheeks, though wasted, lank, and bare,

Filled like a withered russet-pear

In the vacuum of a glass receiver,

And the snows that seventy winters bring

Melted away in that magic spring.

Such, at least, was the wondrous news

The Padre brought into Santa Cruz.

The Church, of course, had its own views

Of who were worthiest to use

The magic spring; but the prior claim

Fell to the aged, sick, and lame.

Far and wide the people came:

Some from the healthful Aptos creek

Hastened to bring their helpless sick;

Even the fishers of rude Soquel

Suddenly found they were far from well;

The brawny dwellers of San Lorenzo

Said, in fact, they had never been so:

5

And all were ailing, — strange to say, —

From Pescadero to Monterey.

Over the mountain they poured in

With leathern bottles, and bags of skin ;

Through the cañons a motley throng

Trotted, hobbled, and limped along.

The fathers gazed at the moving scene

With pious joy and with souls serene ;

And then — a result perhaps foreseen —

They laid out the Mission of San Joaquin.

Not in the eyes of Faith alone

The good effects of the waters shone ;

But skins grew rosy, eyes waxed clear,

Of rough vacquero and muleteer ;

Angular forms were rounded out,

Limbs grew supple, and waists grew stout;

And as for the girls, — for miles about

They had no equal!   To this day,

From Pescadero to Monterey,

You'll still find eyes in which are seen

The liquid graces of San Joaquin.

There is a limit to human bliss,

And the Mission of San Joaquin had this;

None went abroad to roam or stay,

But they fell sick in the queerest way, —

A singular *maladie du pays*,

With gastric symptoms: so they spent

Their days in a sensuous content ;

Caring little for things unseen

Beyond their bowers of living green, —

Beyond the mountains that lay between

The world and the Mission of San Joaquin.

Winter passed, and the summer came:

The trunks of *madroño* all aflame,

Here and there through the underwood

Like pillars of fire starkly stood.

All of the breezy solitude

Was filled with the spicing of pine and bay

And resinous odors mixed and blended,

And dim and ghost-like far away

The smoke of the burning woods ascended.

Then of a sudden the mountains swam,

The rivers piled their floods in a dam

5*

The ridge above Los Gatos creek

   Arched its spine in a feline fashion ;

The forests waltzed till they grew sick,

   And Nature shook in a speechless passion ;

And, swallowed up in the earthquake's spleen,

The wonderful Spring of San Joaquin

Vanished, and never more was seen !

Two days passed : the Mission folk

Out of their rosy dream awoke.

Some of them looked a trifle white ;

But that, no doubt, was from earthquake fright.

Three days : there was sore distress,

Headache, nausea, giddiness.

Four days : faintings, tenderness

Of the mouth and fauces ; and in less

Than one week, — here the story closes ;

We won't continue the prognosis, —

Enough that now no trace is seen

Of Spring or Mission of San Joaquin.

MORAL.

You see the point ? Don't be too quick

To break bad habits : better stick,

Like the Mission folk, to your *arsenic*.

ON A CONE OF THE BIG TREES.

Sequoia Gigantea.

BROWN foundling of the Western wood,
    Babe of primeval wildernesses!
Long on my table thou hast stood
    Encounters strange and rude caresses;
Perchance contented with thy lot,
    Surroundings new and curious faces,
As though ten centuries were not
    Imprisoned in thy shining cases!

Thou bring'st me back the halcyon days

   Of grateful rest; the week of leisure,

The journey lapped in autumn haze,

   The sweet fatigue that seemed a pleasure,

The morning ride, the noonday halt,

   The blazing slopes, the red dust rising,

And then — the dim, brown, columned vault,

   With its cool, damp, sepulchral spicing.

Once more I see the rocking masts

   That scrape the sky, their only tenant

The jay-bird that in frolic casts

   From some high yard his broad blue pennant.

I see the Indian files that keep

   Their places in the dusty heather,

Their red trunks standing ankle deep

   In moccasins of rusty leather.

I see all this, and marvel much
　　That thou, sweet woodland waif, art able
To keep the company of such
　　As throng thy friend's — the poet's — table:
The latest spawn the press hath cast, —
　　The " modern Pope's," " the later Byron's," —
Why e'en the best may not outlast
　　Thy poor relation, — *Sempervirens.*

Thy sire saw the light that shone
　　On Mohammed's uplifted crescent,
On many a royal gilded throne
　　And deed forgotten in the present;
He saw the age of sacred trees
　　And Druid groves and mystic larches;
And saw from forest domes like these
　　The builder bring his Gothic arches.

And must thou, foundling, still forego

    Thy heritage and high ambition,

To lie full lowly and full low,

    Adjusted to thy new condition?

Not hidden in the drifted snows,

    But under ink-drops idly spattered,

And leaves ephemeral as those

    That on thy woodland tomb were scattered.

Yet lie thou there, O friend! and speak

    The moral of thy simple story:

Though life is all that thou dost seek,

    And age alone thy crown of glory, —

Not thine the only germs that fail

    The purpose of their high creation,

If their poor tenements avail

    For worldly show and ostentation.

A SANITARY MESSAGE.

LAST night, above the whistling wind,

    I heard the welcome rain, —

A fusillade upon the roof,

    A tattoo on the pane :

The key-hole piped ; the chimney-top

    A warlike trumpet blew ;

Yet, mingling with these sounds of strife,

    A softer voice stole through.

"Give thanks, O brothers!" said the voice,
"That He who sent the rains
Hath spared your fields the scarlet dew
That drips from patriot veins:
I've seen the grass on Eastern graves
In brighter verdure rise;
But, oh! the rain that gave it life
Sprang first from human eyes.

"I come to wash away no stain
Upon your wasted lea;
I raise no banners, save the ones
The forest wave to me:
Upon the mountain side, where Spring
Her farthest picket sets,
My reveillé awakes a host
Of grassy bayonets.

" I visit every humble roof;

   I mingle with the low:

Only upon the highest peaks

   My blessings fall in snow;

Until, in tricklings of the stream

   And drainings of the lea,

My unspent bounty comes at last

   To mingle with the sea."

And thus all night, above the wind,

   I heard the welcome rain, —

A fusillade upon the roof,

   A tattoo on the pane:

The key-hole piped; the chimney-top

   A warlike trumpet blew;

But, mingling with these sounds of strife,

   This hymn of peace stole through.

6

THE COPPERHEAD.

(1864.)

THERE is peace in the swamp where the Copperhead sleeps,

Where the waters are stagnant, the white vapor
 creeps,

Where the musk of Magnolia hangs thick in the
 air,

And the lilies' phylacteries broaden in prayer;

There is peace in the swamp, though the quiet
 is Death,

Though the mist is miasm, the Upas tree's
 breath,

Though no echo awakes to the cooing of doves, —

There is peace: yes, the peace that the Copperhead loves!

Go seek him: he coils in the ooze and the drip

Like a thong idly flung from the slave-driver's
whip;

But beware the false footstep, — the stumble that
brings

A deadlier lash than the overseer swings.

Never arrow so true, never bullet so dread,

As the straight steady stroke of that hammer-
shaped head;

Whether slave, or proud planter, who braves that
dull crest,

Woe to him who shall trouble the Copperhead's
rest!

Then why waste your labors, brave hearts and

    strong men,

In tracking a trail to the Copperhead's den ?

Lay your axe to the cypress, hew open the shade

To the free sky and sunshine Jehovah has made;

Let the breeze of the North sweep the vapors

    away,

Till the stagnant lake ripples, the freed waters

    play ;

And then to your heel can you righteously doom

The Copperhead born of its shadow and gloom !

ON A PEN OF THOMAS STARR KING.

THIS is the reed the dead musician dropped,

   With tuneful magic in its sheath still hidden;

The prompt allegro of its music stopped,

   Its melodies unbidden.

But who shall finish the unfinished strain,

   Or wake the instrument to awe and wonder,

And bid the slender barrel breathe again, —

   An organ-pipe of thunder?

His pen! what humbler memories cling about
   Its golden curves! what shapes and laughing
      graces
Slipped from its point, when his full heart went out
   In smiles and courtly phrases!

The truth, half jesting, half in earnest flung;
   The word of cheer, with recognition in it;
The note of alms, whose golden speech outrung
   The golden gift within it.

But all in vain the enchanter's wand we wave:
   No stroke of ours recalls his magic vision;
The incantation that its power gave
   Sleeps with the dead magician.

LONE MOUNTAIN.

(CEMETERY, SAN FRANCISCO.)

This is that hill of awe

That Persian Sindbad saw, —

The mount magnetic;

And on its seaward face,

Scattered along its base,

The wrecks prophetic.

Here come the argosies

Blown by each idle breeze,

To and fro shifting;

67

Yet to the hill of Fate
All drawing, soon or late, —
    Day by day drifting ; —

Drifting forever here
Barks that for many a year
    Braved wind and weather ;
Shallops but yesterday
Launched on yon shining bay, —
    Drawn all together.

This is the end of all :
Sun thyself by the wall,
    O poorer Hindbad !
Envy not Sindbad's fame :
Here come alike the same,
    Hindbad and Sindbad.

CALIFORNIA'S GREETING TO SEWARD.

(1869.)

WE know him well: no need of praise
   Or bonfire from the windy hill
To light to softer paths and ways
   The world-worn man we honor still;

No need to quote those truths he spoke
   That burned through years of war and shame,
While History carves with surer stroke
   Across our map his noon-day fame;

No need to bid him show the scars

Of blows dealt by the Scæan gate,

Who lived to pass its shattered bars,

And 'see the foe capitulate;

Who lived to turn his slower feet

Toward the western setting sun,

To see his harvest all complete,

His dream fulfilled, his duty done, —

The one flag streaming from the pole,

The one faith borne from sea to sea, —

For such a triumph, and such goal,

Poor must our human greeting be.

Ah! rather that the conscious land

In simpler ways salute the Man, —

The tall pines bowing where they stand,

   The bared head of El Capitan,

The tumult of the waterfalls,

   Pohono's kerchief in the breeze,

The waving from the rocky walls,

   The stir and rustle of the trees ;

Till lapped in sunset skies of hope,

   In sunset lands by sunset seas,

The Young World's Premier treads the slope

   Of sunset years in calm and peace.

THE TWO SHIPS.

As I stand by the cross on the lone mountain's crest,

    Looking over the ultimate sea,

In the gloom of the mountain a ship lies at rest,

    And one sails away from the lea:

One spreads its white wings on a far-reaching track,

    With pennant and sheet flowing free;

One hides in the shadow with sails laid aback; —

    The ship that is waiting for me!

But lo, in the distance the clouds break away!

   The Gate's glowing portals I see;

And I hear from the outgoing ship in the bay

   The song of the sailors in glee:

So I think of the luminous footprints that bore

   The comfort o'er dark Galilee,

And wait for the signal to go to the shore,

   To the ship that is waiting for me.

THE GODDESS.

FOR THE SANITARY FAIR.

"Who comes?" The sentry's warning cry
  Rings sharply on the evening air:
Who comes? The challenge: no reply,
  Yet something motions there.

A woman, by those graceful folds;
  A soldier, by that martial tread:
"Advance three paces. Halt! until
  Thy name and rank be said."

74

"My name? Her name, in ancient song,
  Who fearless from Olympus came:
Look on me! Mortals know me best
  In battle and in flame."

"Enough! I know that clarion voice;
  I know that gleaming eye and helm;
Those crimson lips, — and in their dew
  The best blood of the realm.

"The young, the brave, the good and wise,
  Have fallen in thy curst embrace:
The juices of the grapes of wrath
  Still stain thy guilty face.

"My brother lies in yonder field,
  Face downward to the quiet grass:

Go back! he cannot see thee now;

But here thou shalt not pass."

A crack upon the evening air,

A wakened echo from the hill:

The watch-dog on the distant shore

Gives mouth, and all is still.

The sentry with his brother lies

Face downward on the quiet grass;

And by him, in the pale moonshine,

A shadow seems to pass.

No lance or warlike shield it bears:

A helmet in its pitying hands

Brings water from the nearest brook,

To meet his last demands.

Can this be she of haughty mien,

   The goddess of the sword and shield?

Ah, yes! The Grecian poet's myth

   Sways still each battle-field.

For not alone that rugged war

   Some grace or charm from beauty gains;

But, when the goddess' work is done,

   The woman's still remains.

ADDRESS.

OPENING OF THE CALIFORNIA THEATRE, SAN FRAN-
CISCO, JAN. 19, 1870.

BRIEF words, when actions wait, are well :

The prompter's hand is on his bell ;

The coming heroes, lovers, kings,

Are idly lounging at the wings ;

Behind the curtain's mystic fold

The glowing future lies unrolled, —

And yet, one moment for the Past ;

One retrospect, — the first and last.

78

"The world's a stage," the master said.

To-night a mightier truth is read :

Not in the shifting canvas screen,

The flash of gas, or tinsel sheen ;

Not in the skill whose signal calls

From empty boards baronial halls ;

But, fronting sea and curving bay,

Behold the players and the play.

Ah, friends ! beneath your real skies

The actor's short-lived triumph dies :

On that broad stage, of empire won

Whose footlights were the setting sun,

Whose flats a distant background rose

In trackless peaks of endless snows ;

Here genius bows, and talent waits

To copy that but One creates.

Your shifting scenes: the league of sand,

An avenue by ocean spanned;

The narrow beach of straggling tents,

A mile of stately monuments;

Your standard, lo! a flag unfurled,

Whose clinging folds clasp half the world, —

This is your drama, built on facts,

With "twenty years between the acts."

One moment more: if here we raise

The oft-sung hymn of local praise,

Before the curtain facts must sway;

Here waits the moral of your play.

Glassed in the poet's thought, you view

What *money* can, yet cannot do;

The faith that soars, the deeds that shine,

Above the gold that builds the shrine.

And oh! when others take our place,

And Earth's green curtain hides our face,

Ere on the stage, so silent now,

The last new hero makes his bow:

So may our deeds, recalled once more

In Memory's sweet but brief encore,

Down all the circling ages run,

With the world's plaudit of "Well done!"

THE LOST GALLEON.

In sixteen hundred and forty-one,
The regular yearly galleon,
Laden with odorous gums and spice,
India cottons and India rice,
And the richest silks of far Cathay,
Was due at Acapulco Bay.

Due she was, and over-due, —
Galleon, merchandise, and crew,
Creeping along through rain and shine,
Through the tropics, under the line.

The trains were waiting outside the walls,

The wives of sailors thronged the town,

The traders sat by their empty stalls,

And the viceroy himself came down ;

The bells in the tower were all a-trip,

Te Deums were on each father's lip,

The limes were ripening in the sun

For the sick of the coming galleon.

All in vain.   Weeks passed away,

And yet no galleon saw the bay :

India goods advanced in price ;

The governor missed his favorite spice ;

The señoritas mourned for sandal,

And the famous cottons of Coromandel ;

And some for an absent lover lost,

And one for a husband, — Donna Julia,

Wife of the captain, tempest-tossed,

In circumstances so peculiar:

Even the fathers, unawares,

Grumbled a little at their prayers;

And all along the coast that year

Votive candles were scarce and dear.

Never a tear bedims the eye

That time and patience will not dry;

Never a lip is curved with pain

That can't be kissed into smiles again:

And these same truths, as far as I know,

Obtained on the coast of Mexico

More than two hundred years ago,

In sixteen hundred and fifty-one, —

Ten years after the deed was done, —

And folks had forgotten the galleon:

The divers plunged in the Gulf for pearls,

White as the teeth of the Indian girls;

The traders sat by their full bazaars;

The mules with many a weary load,

And oxen, dragging their creaking cars,

Came and went on the mountain road.

Where was the galleon all this while:

Wrecked on some lonely coral isle?

Burnt by the roving sea-marauders,

Or sailing north under secret orders?

Had she found the Anian passage famed,

By lying Moldonado claimed,

8

And sailed through the sixty-fifth degree

Direct to the North Atlantic sea?

Or had she found the "River of Kings,"

Of which De Fonté told such strange things

In sixteen forty? Never a sign,

East or West or under the line,

They saw of the missing galleon ;

Never a sail or plank or chip,

They found of the long-lost treasure-ship,

Or enough to build a tale upon.

But when she was lost, and where and how,

Are the facts we're coming to just now.

Take, if you please, the chart of that day

Published at Madrid, —*por el Rey;*

Look for a spot in the old South Sea,

The hundred and eightieth degree

Longitude, west of Madrid : there,

Under the equatorial glare,

Just where the East and West are one,

You'll find the missing galleon, —

You'll find the " San Gregorio," yet

Riding the seas, with sails all set,

Fresh as upon the very day

She sailed from Acapulco Bay.

How did she get there ? What strange spell

Kept her two hundred yea.·s so well,

Free from decay and mortal taint ?

What ? but the prayers of a patron saint !

A hundred leagues from Manilla town,

The "San Gregorio's" helm came down ;

Round she went on her heel, and not

A cable's length from a galliot

That rocked on the waters, just abreast

Of the galleon's course, which was west-sou-west.

Then said the galleon's commandante,

General Pedro Sobriente

(That was his rank on land and main,

A regular custom of Old Spain),

"My pilot is dead of scurvy: may

I ask the longitude, time, and day?"

The first two given and compared ;

The third, — the commandante stared !

"The *first* of June? I make it second."

Said the stranger, "Then you've wrongly-reckoned;

I make it *first*: as you came this way,

You should have lost — d'ye see — a day;

Lost a day, as plainly see,

On the hundred and eightieth degree."

"Lost a day?" "Yes: if not rude,

When did you make east longitude?"

"On the ninth of May, — our patron's day."

"On the ninth? — *you had no ninth of May!*

Eighth and tenth was there; but stay" —

Too late; for the galleon bore away.

Lost was the day they should have kept,

Lost unheeded and lost unwept;

8*

Lost in a way that made search vain,

Lost in the trackless and boundless main;

Lost like the day of Job's awful curse,

In his third chapter, third and fourth verse;

Wrecked was their patron's only day, —

What would the holy fathers say?

Said the Fray Antonio Estavan,

The galleon's chaplain, — a learned man, —

"Nothing is lost that you can regain:

And the way to look for a thing is plain

To go where you lost it, back again.

Back with your galleon till you see

The hundred and eightieth degree.

Wait till the rolling year goes round,

And there will the missing day be found;

For you'll find — if computation's true —

That sailing *east* will give to you

Not only one ninth of May, but two, —

One for the good saint's present cheer,

And one for the day we lost last year."

Back to the spot sailed the galleon;

Where, for a twelve-month, off and on

The hundred and eightieth degree,

She rose and fell on a tropic sea:

But lo! when it came to the ninth of May,

All of a sudden becalmed she lay

One degree from that fatal spot,

Without the power to move a knot;

And of course the moment she lost her way,

Gone was her chance to save that day.

. To cut a lengthening story short,

She never saved it. Made the sport

Of evil spirits and baffling wind,

She was always before or just behind,

One day too soon, or one day too late,

And the sun, meanwhile, would never wait:

She had two eighths, as she idly lay,

Two tenths, but never a *ninth* of May;

And there she rides through two hundred years

Of dreary penance and anxious fears:

Yet through the grace of the saint she served,

Captain and crew are still preserved.

By a computation that still holds good,

Made by the Holy Brotherhood,

The " San Gregorio " will cross that line

In nineteen hundred and thirty-nine:

Just three hundred years to a day

From the time she lost the ninth of May.

And the folk in Acapulco town,

Over the waters, looking down,

Will see in the glow of the setting sun

The sails of the missing galleon,

And the royal standard of Philip *Rey;*

The gleaming mast and glistening spar,

As she nears the surf of the outer bar.

A *Te Deum* sung on her crowded deck,

An odor of spice along the shore,

A crash, a cry from a shattered wreck, —

And the yearly galleon sails no more,

In or out of the olden bay ;

For the blessed patron has found his day.

———

Such is the legend.   Hear this truth :

Over the trackless past, somewhere,

Lie the lost days of our tropic youth,

Only regained by faith and prayer,

Only recalled by prayer and plaint :

Each lost day has its patron saint !

A SECOND REVIEW OF THE GRAND ARMY.

I READ last night of the Grand Review

In Washington's chiefest avenue, —

Two Hundred Thousand men in blue,

    I think they said was the number, —

Till I seemed to hear their trampling feet,

The bugle blast and the drum's quick beat,

The clatter of hoofs in the stony street,

The cheers of people who came to greet,

And the thousand details that to repeat

    Would only my verse encumber, —

Till I fell in a reverie, sad and sweet,

    And then to a fitful slumber.

When, lo ! in a vision I seemed to stand

In the lonely Capitol.   On each hand

Far stretched the portico, dim and grand

Its columns ranged like a martial band

Of sheeted spectres, whom some command

      Had called to a last reviewing.

And the streets of the city were white and bare ;

No footfall echoed across the square ;

But out of the misty midnight air

I heard in the distance a trumpet blare,

And the wandering night-winds seemed to bear

      The sound of a far tattooing.

Then I held my breath with fear and dread ;

For into the square, with a brazen tread,

There rode a figure whose stately head

      O'erlooked the review that morning,

That never bowed from its firm-set seat

When the living column passed its feet,

Yet now rode steadily up the street

  To the phantom bugle's warning:

Till it reached the Capitol square, and wheeled,

And there in the moonlight stood revealed

A well-known form that in State and field

  Had led our patriot sires ;

Whose face was turned to the sleeping camp,

Afar through the river's fog and damp,

That showed no flicker, nor waning lamp,

  Nor wasted bivouac fires.

And I saw a phantom army come,

With never a sound of fife or drum,

But keeping time to a throbbing hum

  Of wailing and lamentation :

9

The martyred heroes of Malvern Hill,

Of Gettysburg and Chancellorsville,

The men whose wasted figures fill

    The patriot graves of the nation.

And there came the nameless dead, — the men

Who perished in fever swamp and fen,

The slowly-starved of the prison-pen ;

    And, marching beside the others,

Came the dusky martyrs of Pillow's fight,

With limbs enfranchised and bearing bright ;

I thought — perhaps 'twas the pale moonlight —

    They looked as white as their brothers !

And so all night marched the Nation's dead

With never a banner above them spread,

Nor a badge, nor a motto brandishèd;

No mark — save the bare uncovered head

    Of the silent bronze Reviewer;

With never an arch save the vaulted sky;

With never a flower save those that lie

On the distant graves — for love could buy

    No gift that was purer or truer.

So all night long swept the strange array,

So all night long till the morning gray

I watched for-one who had passed away,

    With a reverent awe and wonder, —

Till a blue cap waved in the length'ning line,

And I knew that one who was kin of mine

Had come; and I spake — and lo! that sign

    Awakened me from my slumber.

PART II.

BEFORE THE CURTAIN.

BEHIND the footlights hangs the rusty baize,
A trifle shabby in the upturned blaze
Of flaring gas, and curious eyes that gaze.

The stage, methinks, perhaps is none too wide,
And hardly fit for royal Richard's stride,
Or Falstaff's bulk, or Denmark's youthful pride.

Ah, well! no passion walks its humble boards;
O'er it no king nor valiant Hector lords:
The simplest skill is all its space affords.

The song and jest, the dance and trifling play,
The local hit at follies of the day,
The trick to pass an idle hour away, —

For these, no trumpets that announce the Moor,
No blast that makes the hero's welcome sure, —
A single fiddle in the overture !

THE STAGE-DRIVER'S STORY.

IT was the stage-driver's story, as he stood with
his back to the wheelers,

Quietly flecking his whip, and turning his quid of
tobacco ;

While on the dusty road, and blent with the rays
of the moonlight,

We saw the long curl of his lash and the juice of
tobacco descending.

"Danger! Sir, I believe you, — indeed, I may say
  on that subject,
You your existence might put to the hazard and
  turn of a wager.
I have seen danger? Oh, no! not me, sir, indeed,
  I assure you:
'Twas only the man with the dog that is sitting
  alone in yon wagon.

It was the Geiger Grade, a mile and a half from
  the summit:
Black as your hat was the night, and never a star
  in the heavens.
Thundering down the grade, the gravel and stones
  we sent flying
Over the precipice side, — a thousand feet plumb to
  the bottom.

Half-way down the grade I felt, sir, a thrilling and

    creaking,

Then a lurch to one side, as we hung on the bank

    of the cañon ;

Then, looking up the road, I saw, in the distance

    behind me,

The off hind wheel of the coach just loosed from

    its axle, and following.

One glance alone I gave, then gathered together

    my ribbons,

Shouted, and flung them, outspread, on the strain-

    ing necks of my cattle ;

Screamed at the top of my voice, and lashed the

    air in my frenzy,

While down the Geiger Grade, on *three* wheels, the

    vehicle thundered.

Speed was our only chance, when again came the
ominous rattle :

Crack, and another wheel slipped away, and was
lost in the darkness.

Two only now were left ; yet such was our fearful
momentum,

Upright, erect, and sustained on *two* wheels, the
vehicle thundered.

As some huge bowlder, unloosed from its rocky
shelf on the mountain,

Drives before it the hare and the timorous squirrel,
far-leaping,

So down the Geiger Grade rushed the Pioneer
coach, and before it

Leaped the wild horses, and shrieked in advance of
the danger impending.

But to be brief in my tale. Again, ere we came
to the level,

Slipped from its axle a wheel; so that, to be plain
in my statement,

A matter of twelve hundred yards or more, as the
distance may be,

We travelled upon *one* wheel, until we drove up to
the station.

Then, sir, we sank in a heap; but, picking myself
from the ruins,

I heard a noise up the grade; and looking, I saw
in the distance

The three wheels following still, like moons on the
horizon whirling,

Till, circling, they gracefully sank on the road at
the side of the station.

This is my story, sir ; a trifle, indeed, I assure
    you.

Much more, perchance, might be said ; but I hold
    him, of all men, most lightly

Who swerves from the truth in his tale — No, thank
    you — Well, since you *are* pressing,

Perhaps I don't care if I do : you may give me
    the same, Jim, — no sugar."

ASPIRING MISS DE LAINE.

A CHEMICAL NARRATIVE.

CERTAIN facts which serve to explain

The physical charms of Miss Addie De Laine,

Who, as the common reports obtain,

Surpassed in complexion the lily and rose ;

With a very sweet mouth and a *retroussé* nose ;

A figure like Hebe's, or that which revolves

In a milliner's window, and partially solves

That question which mentor and moralist pains,

If grace may exist *minus* feeling or brains.

Of course the young lady had beaux by the
    score,

All that she wanted, — what girl could ask more?

Lovers that sighed, and lovers that swore,

Lovers that danced, and lovers that played,

Men of profession, of leisure, and trade;

But one, who was destined to take the high part

Of holding that mythical treasure, her heart, —

This lover — the wonder and envy of town —

Was a practising chemist, — a fellow called Brown.

I might here remark that 'twas doubted by many,

In regard to the heart, if Miss Addie had any;

But no one could look in that eloquent face,

With its exquisite outline, and features of grace,

And mark, through the transparent skin, how the
tide

Ebbed and flowed at the impulse of passion or
pride, —

None could look, who believed in the blood's cir-
culation

As argued by Harvey, but saw confirmation,

That here, at least, Nature had triumphed o'er art,

And, as far as complexion went, she had a heart.

But this, *par parenthesis.* Brown was the man

Preferred of all others to carry her fan,

Hook her glove, drape her shawl, and do all that a
belle

May demand of the lover she wants to treat well.

10*

Folks wondered and stared that a fellow called
    Brown —

Abstracted and solemn, in manner a clown,

Ill dressed, with a lingering smell of the shop —

Should appear as her escort at party or hop.

Some swore he had cooked up some villanous
    charm,

Or love philter, not in the regular Pharm-

Acopea, and thus, from pure *malis prepense,*

Had bewitched and bamboozled the young lady's
    sense ;

Others thought, with more reason, the secret to lie

In a magical wash or indelible dye ;

While Society, with its censorious eye

And judgment impartial, stood ready to damn

What wasn't improper as being a sham.

For a fortnight the townfolk had all been agog

With a party, the finest the season had seen,

To be given in honor of Miss Pollywog,

Who was just coming out as a belle of sixteen.

The guests were invited : but one night before,

A carriage drew up at the modest back-door

Of Brown's lab'ratory ; and, full in the glare

Of a big purple bottle, some closely-veiled fair

Alighted and entered : to make matters plain,

Spite of veils and disguises, — 'twas Addie De
    Laine.

As a bower for true love, 'twas hardly the one

That a lady would choose to be wooed in or won :

No odor of rose or sweet jessamine's sigh

Breathed a fragrance to hallow their pledge of troth
    by,

Nor the balm that exhales from the odorous thyme;

But the gaseous effusions of chloride of lime,

And salts, which your chemist delights to explain

As the base of the smell of the rose and the drain.

Think of this, O ye lovers of sweetness! and know

What you smell, when you snuff up Lubin or Pi-

naud.

I pass by the greetings, the transports and bliss,

Which, of course, duly followed a meeting like this,

And come down to business; — for such the intent

Of the lady who now o'er the crucible leant,

In the glow of a furnace of carbon and lime,

Like a fairy called up in the new pantomime; —

And give but her words as she coyly looked down,

In reply to the questioning glances of Brown:

"I am taking the drops, and am using the paste,

And the little white powders that had a sweet

    taste,

Which you told me would brighten the glance of

    my eye,

And the depilatory, and also the dye,

And I'm charmed with the trial; and now, my

    dear Brown,

I have one other favor, — now, ducky, don't frown, —

Only one, for a chemist and genius like you

But a trifle, and one you can easily do.

Now listen: to-morrow, you know, is the night

Of the birthday *soireé* of that Pollywog fright;

And I'm to be there, and the dress I shall

    wear

Is *too* lovely; but" — "But what then, *ma chère?*"

Said Brown, as the lady came to a full stop,

And glanced round the shelves of the little back

    shop.

"Well, I want — I want something to fill out the

    skirt

To the proper dimension, without being girt

In a stiff crinoline, or caged in a hoop

That shows through one's skirt like the bars of a

    coop ;

Something light, that a lady may waltz in, or

    polk,

With a freedom that none but you masculine

    folk

Ever know. For, however poor woman aspires,

She's always bound down to the earth by these

    —   wires.

Are you listening? nonsense! don't stare like a
  spoon,

Idiotic; some light thing, and spacious, and
  soon —

Something like — well, in fact — something like a
  balloon!"

Here she paused; and here Brown, overcome by
  surprise,

Gave a doubting assent with still wondering eyes,

And the lady departed. But just at the door

Something happened, — 'tis true, it had happened
  before

In this sanctum of science, — a sibilant sound,

Like some element just from its trammels un-
  bound,

Or two substances that their affinities found.

The night of the anxiously looked-for *soirée*

Had come, with its fair ones in gorgeous array;

With the rattle of wheels, and the tinkle of bells,

And the " How do ye dos," and the " Hope you

    are wells ;'

And the crash in the passage, and last lingering

    look

You give as you hang your best hat on the hook;

The rush of hot air as the door opens wide;

And your entry,— that blending of self-possessed

    pride

And humility shown in your perfect-bred stare

At the folk, as if wondering how they got there;

With other tricks worthy of Vanity Fair.

Meanwhile that safe topic, the heat of the room,

Already was losing its freshness and bloom;

Young people were yawning, and wondering when

The dance would come off, and why didn't it then :

When a vague expectation was thrilling the crowd,

Lo, the door . swung its hinges with utterance

    proud !

And Pompey announced, with a trumpet-like strain,

The entrance of Brown and Miss Addie De Laine.

She entered : but oh, how imperfect the verb

To express to the senses her movement superb !

To say that she "sailed in" more clearly might

    tell

Her grace in its buoyant and billowy swell.

Her robe was a vague circumambient space,

With shadowy boundaries made of point-lace.

11

The rest was but guess-work, and well might
   defy
The power of critical feminine eye
To define or describe : 'twere as futile to try
The gossamer web of the cirrus to trace,
Floating far in the blue of a warm summer sky.

'Midst the humming of praises and the glances of
   beaux,
That greet our fair maiden wherever she goes,
Brown slipped like a shadow, grim, silent, and
   black,
With a look of anxiety, close in her track.
Once he whispered aside in her delicate ear,
A sentence of warning, — it might be of fear :

"Don't stand in a draught, if you value your life."

(Nothing more, — such advice might be given your
    wife

Or your sweetheart, in times of bronchitis and
    cough,

Without mystery, romance, or frivolous scoff.)

But hark to the music: the dance has begun.

The closely-draped windows wide open are flung;

The notes of the piccolo, joyous and light,

Like bubbles burst forth on the warm summer
    night.

Round about go the dancers; in circles they fly;

Trip, trip, go their feet as their skirts eddy by;

And swifter and lighter, but somewhat too plain,

Whisks the fair circumvolving Miss Addie De
    Laine.

Taglioni and Cerito well might have pined

For the vigor and ease that her movements com-

    bined ;

E'en Rigelboche never flung higher her robe

In the naughtiest city that's known on the globe.

'Twas amazing, 'twas scandalous : lost in sur-

    prise,

Some opened their mouths, and a few shut their

    eyes.

But hark ! At the moment Miss Addie De Laine,

Circling round at the outer edge of an ellipse,

Which brought her fair form to the window again,

From the arms of her partner incautiously slips !

And a shriek fills the air, and the music is still,

And the crowd gather round where her partner
forlorn

Still frenziedly points from the wide window-sill

Into space and the night; for Miss Addie was
gone !

Gone like the bubble that bursts in the sun ;

Gone like the grain when the reaper is done ;

Gone like the dew on the fresh morning grass ;

Gone without parting farewell; and alas !

Gone with a flavor of Hydrogen Gas.

. . . .

When the weather is pleasant, you frequently meet

A white-headed man slowly pacing the street ;

His trembling hand shading his lack-lustre eye,

Half blind with continually scanning the sky.

Rumor points him as some astronomical sage,

Reperusing by day the celestial page ;

But the reader, sagacious, will recognize Brown,

Trying vainly to conjure his lost sweetheart down,

And learn the stern moral this story must teach,

That Genius may lift its love out of its reach.

CALIFORNIA MADRIGAL.

ON THE APPROACH OF SPRING.

Oh COME, my beloved! from thy winter abode,

From thy home on the Yuba, thy ranch overflowed:

For the waters have fallen, the winter has fled,

And the river once more has returned to its bed.

Oh, mark how the spring in its beauty is near!

How the fences and tules once more re-appear!

How soft lies the mud on the banks of yon slough

By the hole in the levee the waters broke through!

All Nature, dear Chloris, is blooming to greet

The glance of your eye, and the tread of your feet ;

For the trails are all open, the roads are all free,

And the highwayman's whistle is heard on the lea.

Again swings the lash on the high mountain trail,

And the pipe of the packer is scenting the gale ;

The·oath and the jest ringing high o'er the plain,

Where the smut is not always confined to the grain

Once more glares the sunlight on awning and roof,

Once more the red clay's pulverized by the hoof,

Once more the dust powders the "outsides" with red,

Once more at the station the whiskey is spread.

Then fly with me, love, ere the summer's begun,

And the mercury mounts to one hundred and one;

Ere the grass now so green shall be withered and sear,

In the spring that obtains but one month in the year.

ST. THOMAS.

(1868.)

VERY fair and full of promise

Lay the island of St. Thomas:

Ocean o'er its reefs and bars

Hid its elemental scars;

Groves of cocoanut and guava

Grew above its fields of lava.

So the gem of the Antilles, —

"Isles of Eden," where no ill is, —

Like a great green turtle slumbered

On the sea that it encumbered.

Then said William Henry Seward,

As he cast his eye to leeward,

" Quite important to our commerce

Is this island of St. Thomas."

Said the Mountain ranges, " Thank'ee,

But we cannot stand the Yankee

O'er our scars and fissures poring,

In our very vitals boring,

· In our sacred caverns prying,

All our secret problems trying, —

Digging, blasting, with dynamit

Mocking all our thunders ! Damn it !

Other lands may be more civil,

Bust our lava crust if we will."

Said the Sea, — its white teeth gnashing

Through its coral-reef lips flashing, —

"Shall I let this scheming mortal

Shut with stone my shining portal,

Curb my tide, and check my play,

Fence with wharves my shining bay?

Rather let me be drawn out

In one awful water-spout!"

Said the black-browed Hurricane,

Brooding down the Spanish main,

"Shall I see my forces, zounds!

Measured by square inch and pounds,

With detectives at my back

When I double on my track,

And my secret paths made clear,

Published o'er the hemisphere

To each gaping, prying crew?

Shall I?   Blow me if I do!"

So the Mountains shook and thundered,

And the Hurricane came sweeping,

And the people stared and wondered

As the Sea came on them leaping:

Each, according to his promise,

Made things lively at St. Thomas.

Till one morn, when Mr. Seward

Cast his weather eye to leeward,

There was not an inch of dry land

Left to mark his recent island.

12

Not a flagstaff or a sentry,

Not a wharf or port of entry, —

Only — to cut matters shorter —

Just a patch of muddy water

In the open ocean lying,

And a gull above it flying.

THE BALLAD OF MR. COOKE.

A LEGEND OF THE CLIFF HOUSE, SAN FRANCISCO.

WHERE the sturdy ocean breeze

Drives the spray of roaring seas

That the Cliff-House balconies

                Overlook :

There, in spite of rain that balked,

With his sandals duly chalked,

Once upon a tight-rope walked

                Mr. Cooke.

But the jester's lightsome mien,

And his spangles and his sheen,

All had vanished, when the scene

            He forsook; ——

Yet in some delusive hope,

In some vague desire to cope,

One still came to view the rope

            Walked by Cooke.

.   .   .   .   .   .

Amid Beauty's bright array,

On that strange eventful day,

Partly hidden from the spray,

            In a nook,

Stood Florinda Vere de Vere;

Who with wind-dishevelled hair,

And a rapt, distracted air,

            Gazed on Cooke.

Then she turned, and quickly cried

To her lover at her side,

While her form with love and pride

     Wildly shook,

"Clifford Snook! oh, hear me now!

Here I break each plighted vow:

There's but one to whom I bow,

     And that's Cooke!"

Haughtily that young man spoke:

"I descend from noble folk.

'Seven Oaks,' and then 'Se'nnoak,'

     Lastly Snook,

Is the way my name I trace:

Shall a youth of noble race

In affairs of love give place

     To a Cooke?"

12*

"Clifford Snook, I know thy claim

To that lineage and name,

And I think I've read the same

              In Horne Tooke;

But I swear, by all divine,

Never, never to be thine,

'Till thou canst upon yon line

              Walk like Cooke."

Though to that gymnastic feat

He no closer might compete

Than to strike a *balance*-sheet

              In a book;

Yet thenceforward, from that day,

He his figure would display

In some wild athletic way,

              After Cooke.

On some household eminence,

On a clothes-line or a fence,

Over ditches, drains, and thence

       O'er a brook,

He, by high ambition led,

Ever walked and balancèd;

Till the people, wondering, said,

       "How like Cooke!"

Step by step did he proceed,

Nerved by valor, not by greed,

And at last the crowning deed

       Undertook:

Misty was the midnight air,

And the cliff was bleak and bare,

When he came to do and dare

       Just like Cooke.

Through the darkness, o'er the flow,

Stretched the line where he should go

Straight across, as flies the crow

          Or the rook :

One wild glance around he cast ;

Then he faced the ocean blast,

And he strode the cable last

          Touched by Cooke.

Vainly roared the angry seas ;

Vainly blew the ocean breeze ;

But, alas ! the walker's knees

          Had a crook ;

And before he reached the rock

Did they both together knock,

And he stumbled with a shock —

          Unlike Cooke !

Downward dropping in the dark,

Like an arrow to its mark,

Or a fish-pole when a shark

            Bites the hook,

Dropped the pole he could not save,

Dropped the walker, and the wave

Swift ingulfed the rival brave

            Of J. Cooke!

Came a roar across the sea

Of sea-lions in their glee,

In a tongue remarkably

            Like Chinnook ;

And the maddened sea-gull seemed

Still to utter, as he screamed,

" Perish thus the wretch who deemed

            Himself Cooke ! "

But, on misty moonlit nights,

Comes a skeleton in tights,

Walks once more the giddy heights

    He mistook;

And unseen to mortal eyes,

Purged of grosser earthly ties,

Now at last in spirit guise

    Outdoes Cooke.

. . . . . .

Still the sturdy ocean breeze

Sweeps the spray of roaring seas,

Where the Cliff-House balconies

    Overlook;

And the maidens in their prime,

Reading of this mournful rhyme,

Weep where, in the olden time,

    Walked J. Cooke.

THE LEGENDS OF THE RHINE.

BEETLING walls with ivy grown,

Frowning heights of mossy stone ;

Turret, with its flaunting flag

Flung from battlemented crag ;

Dungeon-keep and fortalice

Looking down a precipice

O'er the darkly glancing wave

By the Lurline-haunted cave ;

Robber haunt and maiden bower,

Home of Love and Crime and Power, —

That's the scenery, in fine,

Of the Legends of the Rhine.

One bold baron, double-dyed

Bigamist and parricide,

And, as most the stories run,

Partner of the Evil One;

Injured innocence in white,

Fair but idiotic quite,

Wringing of her lily hands ;

Valor fresh from Paynim lands,

Abbot ruddy, hermit pale,

Minstrel fraught with many a tale, —

Are the actors that combine

In the Legends of the Rhine.

Bell-mouthed flagons round a board ;

Suits of armor, shield, and sword ;

Kerchief with its bloody stain ;

Ghosts of the untimely slain ;

Thunder-clap and clanking chain ;

Headsman's block and shining axe ;

Thumbscrews, crucifixes, racks ;

Midnight-tolling chapel bell,

Heard across the gloomy fell, —

These, and other pleasant facts,

Are the properties that shine

In the Legends of the Rhine.

Maledictions, whispered vows

Underneath the linden boughs ;

Murder, bigamy, and theft ;

Travellers of goods bereft ;

13

Rapine, pillage, arson, spoil, —

Every thing but honest toil,

Are the deeds that best define

Every Legend of the Rhine.

That Virtue always meets reward,

But quicker when it wears a sword ;

That Providence has special care

Of gallant knight and lady fair ;

That villains, as a thing of course,

Are always haunted by remorse, —

Is the moral, I opine,

Of the Legends of the Rhine.

MRS. JUDGE JENKINS.

[BEING THE ONLY GENUINE SEQUEL TO "MAUD MULLER."]

MAUD MULLER, all that summer day,
Raked the meadow sweet with hay;

Yet, looking down the distant lane,
She hoped the judge would come again.

But when he came, with smile and bow,
Maud only blushed, and stammered, " Ha-ow ? "

147

And spoke of her "pa," and wondered whether

He'd give consent they should wed together.

Old Muller burst in tears, and then

Begged that the judge would lend him "ten;"

For trade was dull, and wages low,

And the "craps," this year, were somewhat slow.

And ere the languid summer died,

Sweet Maud became the judge's bride.

But, on the day that they were mated,

Maud's brother Bob was intoxicated;

And Maud's relations, twelve in all,

Were very drunk at the judge's hall.

And when the summer came again,

The young bride bore him babies twain.

And the judge was blest, but thought it strange

That bearing children made such a change:

For Maud grew broad and red and stout;

And the waist that his arm once clasped about

Was more than he now could span. And he

Sighed as he pondered, ruefully,

How that which in Maud was native grace

In Mrs. Jenkins was out of place;

And thought of the twins, and wished that they

Looked less like the man who raked the hay

13*

On Muller's farm, and dreamed with pain
Of the day he wandered down the lane.

And, looking down that dreary track,
He half regretted that he came back.

For, had he waited, he might have wed
Some maiden fair and thoroughbred ;

For there be women fair as she,
Whose verbs and nouns do more agree.

Alas for maiden ! alas for judge !
And the sentimental, — that's one-half "fudge ;"

For Maud soon thought the judge a bore,
With all his learning and all his lore.

And the judge would have bartered Maud's fair
    face
For more refinement and social grace.

If, of all words of tongue and pen,
The saddest are, " It might have been,"

More sad are these we daily see :
" It is, but hadn't ought to be."

AVITOR.

AN AERIAL RETROSPECT.

WHAT was it filled my youthful dreams,

In place of Greek or Latin themes,

Or beauty's wild, bewildering beams?

                 Avitor?

What visions and celestial scenes

I filled with aerial machines, —

Montgolfier's and Mr. Green's!

                 Avitor.

What fairy tales seemed things of course!

The rock that brought Sindbad across,

The Calendar's own winged-horse!

Avitor!

How many things I took for facts, —

Icarus and his conduct lax,

And how he sealed his fate with wax!

Avitor!

The first balloons I sought to sail,

Soap-bubbles fair, but all too frail,

Or kites, — but thereby hangs a tail.

Avitor!

What made me launch from attic tall

A kitten and a parasol,

And watch their bitter, frightful fall?

Avitor?

What youthful dreams of high renown

Bade me inflate the parson's gown,

That went not up, nor yet came down?

> Avitor?

My first ascent, I may not tell:

Enough to know that in that well

My first high aspirations fell,

> Avitor!

My other failures let me pass:

The dire explosions; and, alas!

The friends I choked with noxious gas,

> Avitor!

For lo! I see perfected rise

The vision of my boyish eyes,

The messenger of upper skies,

> Avitor!

A WHITE-PINE BALLAD.

RECENTLY with Samuel Johnson this occasion I
improved,
Whereby certain gents of affluence I hear were
greatly moved ;
But not all of Johnson's folly, although multiplied
by nine,
Could compare with Milton Perkins, late an owner
in White Pine.

Johnson's folly — to be candid — was a wild desire

.　to treat

Every able male white citizen he met upon the

street;

And there being several thousand — but this sub-

ject why pursue?

'Tis with Perkins, and not Johnson, that to-day we

have to do.

No: not wild promiscuous treating, not the wine-

cup's ruby flow,

But the female of his species brought the noble

Perkins low.

'Twas a wild poetic fervor, and excess of senti-

ment,

That left the noble Perkins in a week without a

cent.

"Milton Perkins," said the Siren, "not thy wealth
    do I admire,

But the intellect that flashes from those eyes of
    opal fire ;

And methinks the name thou bearest surely can-
    not be misplaced,

And, embrace me, Mister Perkins!" Milton Per-
    kins her embraced.

But I grieve to state, that even then, as she was
    wiping dry

The tear of sensibility in Milton Perkins' eye,

She prigged his diamond bosom-pin, and that her
    wipe of lace

Did seem to have of chloroform a most suspicious
    trace.

14

Enough that Milton Perkins later in the night was
found

With his head in an ash-barrel, and his feet upon
the ground ;

And he murmured "Seraphina," and he kissed his
hand, and smiled

On a party who went through him, like an unre-
sisting child.

MORAL.

Now one word to Pogonippers, ere this subject I
resign,

In this tale of Milton Perkins, — late an owner in
White Pine, —

You shall see that wealth and women are deceit-
 ful, just the same ;
And the tear of sensibility has salted many a
 claim.

WHAT THE WOLF REALLY SAID TO LITTLE RED RIDING-HOOD.

WONDERING maiden, so puzzled and fair,
Why dost thou murmur and ponder and stare?
"Why are my eyelids so open and wild?" —
Only the better to see with, my child!
Only the better and clearer to view
Cheeks that are rosy, and eyes that are blue.

Dost thou still wonder, and ask why these arms
Fill thy soft bosom with tender alarms,
Swaying so wickedly? — are they misplaced,
Clasping or shielding some delicate waist:

Hands whose coarse sinews may fill you with fear

Only the better protect you, my dear!

Little Red Riding-Hood, when in the street,

Why do I press your small hand when we meet?

Why, when you timidly offered your cheek,

Why did I sigh, and why didn't I speak?

Why, well: you see — if the truth must ap-

 pear —

I'm not your grandmother, Riding-Hood, dear!

14*

THE RITUALIST.

BY A COMMUNICANT OF "ST. JAMES'S."

HE wore, I think, a chasuble, the day when first
we met ;

A stole and snowy alb likewise : I recollect it yet.

He called me "daughter," as he raised his jewelled
hand to bless ;

And then, in thrilling undertones, he asked, " Would
I confess ? "

O mother, dear! blame not your child, if then on
  bended knees

I dropped, and thought of Abelard, and also Eloise;

Or when, beside the altar high, he bowed before
  the pyx,

I envied that seraphic kiss he gave the crucifix.

The cruel world may think it wrong, perhaps may
  deem me weak,

And, speaking of that sainted man, may call his
  conduct "cheek;"

And, like that wicked barrister whom Cousin Har-
  ry quotes,

May term his mixèd chalice "grog," his vestments,
  "petticoats."

But, whatsoe'er they do or say, I'll build a Christian's hope

On incense and on altar-lights, on chasuble and cope.

Let others prove, by precedent, the faith that they profess :

" His can't be wrong " that's symbolized by such becoming dress.

A MORAL VINDICATOR.

If Mr. Jones, Lycurgus B.,
Had one peculiar quality,
'Twas his severe advocacy
Of conjugal fidelity.

His views of heaven were very free;
His views of life were painfully
Ridiculous; but fervently
He dwelt on marriage sanctity.

He frequently went on a spree ;

But in his wildest revelry,

On this especial subject he

Betrayed no ambiguity.

And though at times Lycurgus B.

Did lay his hands not lovingly

Upon his wife, the sanctity

Of wedlock was his guaranty.

But Mrs. Jones declined to see

Affairs in the same light as he,

And quietly got a decree

Divorcing her from that L. B.

And what did Jones, Lycurgus B.,

With his known idiosyncrasy ?

He smiled, — a bitter smile to see, —

And drew the weapon of Bowie

He did what Sickles did to Key, —

What Cole on Hiscock wrought, did he ;

In fact, on persons twenty-three

He proved the marriage sanctity.

The counsellor who took the fee,

The witnesses and referee,

The judge who granted the decree,

Died in that wholesale butchery.

And then when Jones, Lycurgus B.,

Had wiped the weapon of Bowie,

Twelve jurymen did instantly

Acquit and set Lycurgus free.

SONGS WITHOUT SENSE.

FOR THE PARLOR AND PIANO.

I. — THE PERSONIFIED SENTIMENTAL.

AFFECTION's charm no longer gilds

  The idol of the shrine ;

But cold Oblivion seeks to fill

  Regret's ambrosial wine.

Though Friendship's offering buried lies

  'Neath cold Aversion's snow,

Regard and Faith will ever bloom

  Perpetually below.

I see thee whirl in marble halls,

   In Pleasure's giddy train;

Remorse is never on that brow,

   Nor Sorrow's mark of pain.

Deceit has marked thee for her own;

   Inconstancy the same;

And Ruin wildly sheds its gleam

   Athwart thy path of shame.

II.—THE HOMELY PATHETIC.

THE dews are heavy on my brow;

   My breath comes hard and low;

Yet, mother, dear, grant one request,

   Before your boy must go.

15

Oh! lift me ere my spirit sinks,
　And ere my senses fail:
Place me once more, O mother dear!
　Astride the old fence-rail.

The old fence-rail, the old fence-rail!
　How oft these youthful legs,
With Alice' and Ben Bolt's, were hung
　Across those wooden pegs.
'Twas there the nauseating smoke
　Of my first pipe arose:
O mother, dear! these agonies
　Are far less keen than those.

I know where lies the hazel dell,
　Where simple Nellie sleeps;
I know the cot of Nettie Moore,
　And where the willow weeps.

I know the brookside and the mill :

But all their pathos fails

Beside the days when once I sat

Astride the old fence-rails.

III. — SWISS AIR.

I M a gay tra, la, la,

With my fal, lal, la, la,

And my bright —

And my light —

    Tra, la, le.   [Repeat.]

Then laugh, ha, ha, ha,

And ring, ting, ling, ling,

· And sing fal, la, la,

    La, la, le.   [Repeat.]